BRIGHT and EARLY BOOKS for BEGINNING Beginners

This book belongs to …

GROLIER
BOOK CLUB EDITION

BERENSTAINS'
A
BOOK

Published in the United States by Random House, Inc., New York,
and simultaneously in Canada by Random House of Canada Limited, Toronto.

http://www.randomhouse.com/

Library of Congress Cataloging-in-Publication Data
Berenstain, Stan, 1923–
The Berenstains' **A book** / [Stan & Jan Berenstain].
p. cm. — (A bright and early book)
SUMMARY: An army of angry ants march across and around
all sorts of items that begin with the letter "a."
ISBN 0-679-88705-9 (trade). — ISBN 0-679-98705-3 (lib. bdg.)
[1. Ants—Fiction. 2. Alphabet.]
I. Berenstain, Jan, 1923– II. Title. III. Series: Bright and early book.
PZ7.B4483Bfwl 1997 [E]—dc21 97-6783

Printed in the United States of America 10 9 8 7 6 5 4 3 2 1

Stan & Jan Berenstain

A Bright and Early Book
From BEGINNER BOOKS
A Division of Random House, Inc.

Ant

Ants

Angry ants advance

—across an apple,

across an acorn.

Angry ants
advance across
an apple
and an acorn,

across an apricot,

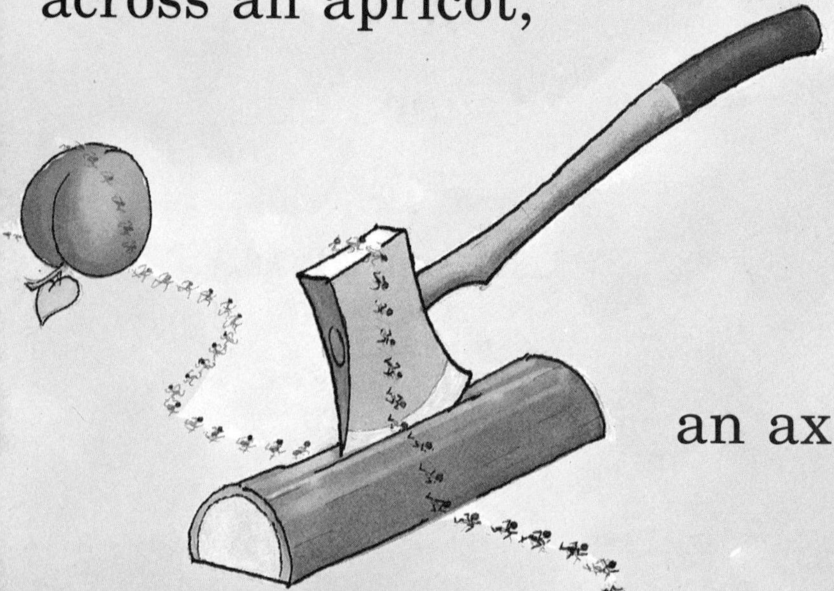

an ax,

and an angleworm.

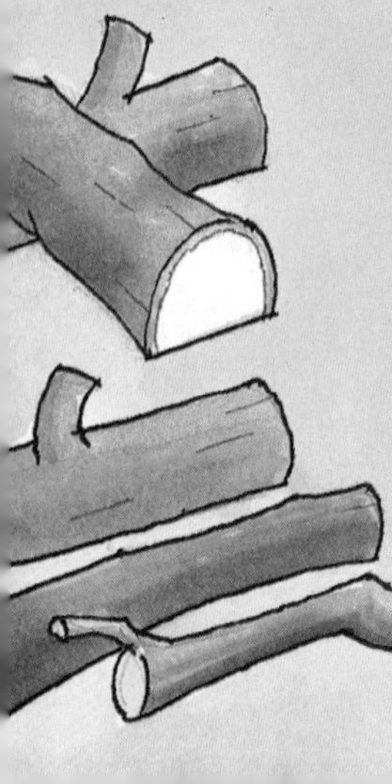

Why do angry ants
advance across
an apple,
an acorn,
an apricot,
an ax,
and an angleworm?

Angry ants
advance across
an alligator

and Aunt Alice's airplane,

and across Avenue A.

Angry ants
advance across
apes' apartments

—and all Arizona!

ARIZONA

ARIZO

Why do angry ants
advance across
an apple,
an acorn,
an apricot,
an ax,
an angleworm,
an alligator,
Aunt Alice's airplane,
Avenue A,
apes' apartments,
and all Arizona?

Aha!
An anteater
and
an anthill!

ATTACK!

A-A-A-R-R!

That's why
angry ants advanced
across an apple,
an acorn,
an apricot,
an ax,
an angleworm,
an alligator,
Aunt Alice's airplane,
Avenue A,
apes' apartments,
and all Arizona!

Ants are amazing.

BRIGHT and EARLY BOOKS for BEGINNING Beginners